THIS WALKER BOOK BELONGS TO:

FOR JO

First published 1990 by Walker Books Ltd
87 Vauxhall Walk, London SE11 5HJ

This edition published 1998

© 1990 Chris Riddell

2 4 6 8 10 9 7 5 3

Printed in Hong Kong/China

British Library Cataloguing in Publication Data
A catalogue record for this book is
available from the British Library.

ISBN 0-7445-6078-0

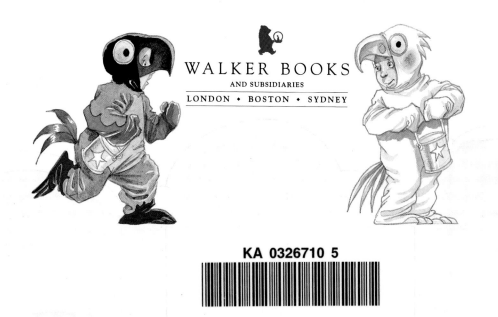

THE
WISH FACTORY

Chris Riddell

WALKER BOOKS
AND SUBSIDIARIES
LONDON • BOSTON • SYDNEY

Oliver used to have
a bad dream about a monster.
But one night a cloud came
instead of the dream...

*and carried Oliver into
the big, blue night...*

far, far away to the Wish Factory.

Oliver closed his eyes and thought a big wish.

Then the wish-makers made it good and strong...

and wrapped it up to keep it fresh.

"We hope it comes true," they said.

Then Oliver was in his own bed
and dreaming…

THE BIG BAD DREAM.

So Oliver untied the ribbon...

and out came the wish ...

and the wish came true.

The monster wasn't big
any more, and it wasn't bad.
"Boo!" said Oliver.

And morning came quite soon.

MORE WALKER PAPERBACKS
For You to Enjoy

THE TROUBLE WITH ELEPHANTS
by Chris Riddell

Full of jolly jumbo jokes, this is a must for "elefans".

"Particularly likeable. It wittily records the many problems that can arise with elephants around, such as their habit of eating all the buns at picnics and taking all the bedclothes at night." *The Sunday Times*

0-7445-5447-0   £4.99

BEN AND THE BEAR
by Chris Riddell

"One of my favourite 'Bear' books…
Good clear sentences suitable for children who have just started the reading habit or like a story read to them."
Belfast Telegraph

0-7445-5271-0   £4.99

KATE'S GIANTS
by Valiska Gregory/Virginia Austin

Kate doesn't like the attic door in her room.
Scary things might come through it, she thinks. There might be wild animals or giants… And, lying in the dark, she's sure there are!

"This book with its warm and intimate illustrations and reassuring text shows how the power of imagination can be used to control fear as well as provoking it." *Baby Magazine*

0-7445-4069-0   £4.99